SKY-HIGH

Other Teenage Mutant Ninja Turtle books available in Yearling Books:

Teenage Mutant Ninja Turtles
    (a novelization of the movie) by B. B. Hiller
Six-Guns and Shurikens by Dave Morris
Red Herrings by Dave Morris
Buried Treasure by Dave Morris

Yearling Books/Young Yearlings/Yearling Classics are designed especially to entertain and enlighten young people. Patricia Reilly Giff, consultant to this series, received the bachelor's degree from Marymount College. She holds the master's degree in history from St. John's University, and a Professional Diploma in Reading from Hofstra University. She was a teacher and reading consultant for many years, and is the author of numerous books for young readers.

For a complete listing of all Yearling titles, write to
Dell Readers Service
P.O. Box 1045
South Holland, IL 60473.

SKY-HIGH

D A V E   M O R R I S

Illustrated by Phil Jacobs

A YEARLING BOOK

Published by
Dell Publishing
a division of
Bantam Doubleday Dell Publishing Group, Inc.
666 Fifth Avenue
New York, New York 10103

This work was first published in Great Britain by Yearling Books,
Transworld Publishers Ltd.

ISBN: 0-440-40389-8

Printed in the United States of America

June 1990

10   9   8   7   6   5

HEROES IN A HALF SHELL

Fourteen years ago a group of four ordinary turtles that had dropped into the storm drains beneath New York were found by Splinter, a master of the skill of ninjutsu, the ancient Japanese art of stealth and espionage.

Then . . . a leakage of radioactive goo exposed Splinter and his pets to mutating chemicals. Splinter turned into a giant talking rat, while the turtles became the Teenage Mutant Ninja Turtles—his wacky, wisecracking, crime-fighting ninja pupils.

With their human friend, April O'Neil, ace reporter on the Channel 6 TV News, the Turtles fight for what's right and foil the nefarious schemes of the Shredder, Splinter's evil renegade student.

Meet Leonardo, the coolly efficient sword-swinging team leader. Meet Donatello, the expert when it comes to machines; his swishing quarterstaff lays out his foes like bowling pins. Meet Raphael, the prankster, whose wry humor sees the team through perilous situations while his twin daggers send enemies fleeing in panic. And meet Michaelangelo, who's a master of the flying kick and the karate punch and is prepared to use them on anyone who gets between him and a pizza!

The four turtles were working out with
Master Splinter in his dojo, or training
room, in the storm drains under New
York. It was here that he put them
through their paces and taught them the
martial arts. Usually he gave them a
hard workout, knowing that their profi-
ciency in these skills might one day save
their lives, to say nothing of the lives of

the ordinary members of the public, whom they were sworn to protect.

Today was no exception. After an hour of grueling exercises, Splinter decided to test his pupils' speed and coordination. He selected a weapon comprising a padded stick attached by a long piece of rope to a weighted ball.

"This is a kusari-gama," he said to the Turtles. "It is a weapon of old Japan, nowadays rarely encountered—but you should know how to deal with it all the same."

"It doesn't look very dangerous to me, master," remarked Michaelangelo, rather bored by the lecture.

Splinter looked sharply at him. "This is just a practice version, Michaelangelo. Naturally it would be much too dangerous to train with the real thing, which consists of an iron ball on a chain."

"Freaky," whispered Raphael to the others. "Wonder who'd use something like that in this day and age, dudes?"

Master Splinter, who had excellent

hearing, caught this remark. "The Shredder would!" he boomed. "There is no weapon or trick too devious for that ignoble villain to use. I should know, my pupils, for I taught him most of them. Now, Donatello, perhaps you'll help me demonstrate."

Like the others, Donatello was faintly bored by these exercises involving old-fashioned traditional weapons. He was more interested in the use of the quarter-staff and in mechanical gadgets. Before he even had time to collect his thoughts, Splinter had darted forward and lunged at him with one end of the padded stick, at the same time swinging the ball around on the end of the rope. Donatello parried instinctively, blocking the stick with his left arm while raising his right hand to fend off the ball. The rope curled around his arm and the ball completed its arc, thudding into the back of his head. It was only made of rubber, but it made Donatello wince.

"You see?" said Splinter. "These old-fashioned tools of the Ninja art still have something to teach a young whippersnapper. In this case never forget that what looks like a frontal assault may well turn out to be a cunning diversion." He looked at the Turtles' blank expressions. "All right. Practice your sparring for an hour and then take the afternoon off."

As the others started to spar, Splinter led Leonardo off to one side. "My son," he said, "I am concerned. It seems that none of you really have your minds on the job today."

Leonardo was Splinter's most dedicated student, but even he felt like taking a rest now and again. "Don't forget, we've been caught up in all kinds of adventures recently," he pointed out.

"A ninja must always be alert," said Splinter flatly. "It is for your own sakes that I drive you so hard, Leonardo."

"But you know what they say about all work and no play, master . . ."

Splinter grinned. "A change is as

good as a rest, eh, Leonardo? Very well, perhaps you're right; sometimes I can be a hard taskmaster." He turned around. "All right, that's enough for one day. Class dismissed."

"Yay!" said Michaelangelo, clicking his heels. "Let's celebrate over a pizza, guys. Who's got the greenbacks?"

"Eh?" said Splinter. "You all have green backs."

"No, master," said Donatello, laughing, "he means dollars—you know, money."

Splinter nodded, still smiling, and reached into his wallet. "Aha, well then, after working you so hard, the least I can do is treat you to one of these, um, pizzas." He handed Michaelangelo some cash. "Go on, Michaelangelo. And make sure you ask for one with all the, er, clippings."

"You mean 'all the trimmings,' master," corrected Michaelangelo. "And you bet I will. Thanks!"

When they returned half an hour

later, though, Splinter cast a dubious eye over their pizza. "Bread coated with melted cheese?"

"That's what a pizza is, master," said Leonardo.

"Well, and there are all the clippings—I mean, trimmings," added Donatello.

"Yeah," said Raphael. "Look, we've got green peppers, onions, salami, mushrooms, anchovies, tomatoes, chili peppers, tuna, pecans, chocolate buttons—"

"Pecans?" said Splinter, raising an eyebrow. *"Chocolate buttons?"*

"Yeah, well . . ." Raphael glanced at the pizza and shrugged. "We made the mistake of letting Mike order."

Splinter gave a sigh. "Whatever you like. I wonder why you don't try a simpler food, my students. Myself, I never feel set up for the day until I've had a nice bowl of sushi and boiled rice washed down with a cup of green tea." He smacked his lips at the thought.

"Green tea?" said Raphael after

Splinter had walked off. "Have you tried the stuff, dudes? It tastes like it's made out of lawn trimmings."

"And sushi?" said Michaelangelo. "That's just raw fish, for pete's sake!"

"Well, I don't know," said Leonardo as he carefully removed the drops of half-melted chocolate from his pizza slice. "Maybe we could make a change just one time, so as to please Master Splinter."

"Leo," said Raphael firmly between munches on his own slice, "I am *not* eating raw fish." The other two nodded in vigorous agreement.

Leonardo chuckled. "Don't worry, dudes, I wasn't thinking of that. But I've thought of a compromise . . ."

◆

"Fish and chips?" said Splinter at suppertime a few days later. He smiled. "It isn't exactly what I had in mind, but it is a step in the right direction at least. A ninja needs sharp wits, and fish is food for the brain, you know." He lifted a piece of fish in his chopsticks and devoured it appreciatively.

"I reckon I prefer food for the stomach," said Michaelangelo with a sigh. To tell the truth, he was quite enjoying the meal—especially the chips—but he missed his customary pizza.

"The only thing wrong with fish and chips," declared Raphael, "is that you can't get it with pepperoni and olives."

"No 'clippings,' eh, Raphael?" said Splinter. He gave a wink to show that he had remembered the proper word, really.

Donatello laughed and pointed to the newspaper wrappings. "Actually, master, you do get clippings of a sort. News clippings."

"I wonder why they wrap fish and chips in newspaper," mused Leonardo.

"Presumably," said Splinter, "it's so that you have something to read while you're eating." He glanced at one of the crumpled bits of paper littering the table and smoothed it out with one hand.

"S-W-E-N Y-L-I-A-D" spelled out Michaelangelo, who was not very good at reading. "Why, that's written upside down!"

"Turn it around, you clot!" said Raphael, grabbing the bit of newspaper that Michaelangelo was looking at.

"What's the headline?" asked Michaelangelo.

Raphael pretended to scrutinize it. "It says, 'Michaelangelo not a Turtle, Shock Horror! Famous Crimebuster really a Mutant Pistachio, say Scientists.' "

Michaelangelo hesitated just long enough for all the others to burst out laughing. "Aww, you just made that up," he said.

Splinter took a glance at the newspaper page. He was just mildly curious as to the real headline, but something else caught his eye that made him do a double take. *"What?"* he cried. He snatched the paper from Raphael's hands and stared intently at it.

"What is it, master?" asked Raphael,

craning his neck to see what had caught Splinter's attention. The others crowded around.

Splinter pointed to a photograph at the bottom of the crumpled page. It showed an astronaut named Colonel Hector Munro. According to the accompanying news report, he was one of three astronauts due to go up on the next shuttle launch to rendezvous with an orbiting space station.

"I don't get it," said Leonardo, after he had read the newspaper story. "What's wrong?"

Splinter pointed at the photo, his finger trembling with rage and horror. "That's no astronaut," he explained. "That's my treacherous ex-pupil, Saki— better known nowadays as the Shredder!"

Leonardo gasped. "Somehow he's wormed his way into the crew of the space shuttle."

"And if he wants to get up into space," said Donatello, speaking what was in everybody's mind, "it's a sure bet that he

• 10 •

has some invidious scheme up his tin-plated sleeve."

Splinter jumped up and raced them to the bay where the Turtle airship was docked. "Hurry, my pupils!" he shouted urgently. "Countless lives might be jeopardized if the Shredder takes over that space station. We have to reach Cape Canaveral before the launch!"

The Turtle airship rose up into the afternoon sunlight, apparently from out of a garbage dump in the middle of an empty lot. In fact the dump concealed an enlarged tunnel down to the storm drains. Normally when it was necessary to use the airship, Splinter would arrange for it to take off at night, when there was nobody around to see. This time the emergency forced him to take risks. Fortunately there were just a couple of children playing in the area. They glanced up, watched the airship for a few moments, then went back to kicking their football around.

Fingers darting over the controls, Splinter turned the airship to point south. Slowly at first, but with increasing speed, they began to move off across the sky.

Donatello looked up from a map on which he had been making some calculations. "We should arrive at Cape Canaveral with about two hours to spare," he announced.

"That should give us plenty of time to warn the people in charge," said Leonardo, nodding.

But Splinter shook his head. "It will not be as easy at that. Do you think the authorities will believe the word of a mutant rat and his four testudinarious pupils?"

"Test tube in *what,* master?" queried Michaelangelo.

"That means 'turtlish,'" said Donatello.

"Except in your case, Mike," put in Raphael, "when it means 'dumb.'"

"Do not make jokes," ordered Splinter sharply. "The situation is very serious, and your minds must be focused. Rest assured that the Shredder will stop at nothing to make sure that his plans succeed. We must stop at nothing to make sure that they don't."

Michaelangelo was gazing out the window. Night had fallen as they sped south, but it was still possible to make out the coastline by the sprinkling of city lights and the gleam of roadways far below. "Master Splinter," he said, "you told us that the Shredder was your pupil once."

Splinter flicked the airship onto automatic pilot, then swiveled around in his chair to address them all. "Yes," he said, "he was a student by the name of Saki at my ninja academy in Japan. One day he hatched a plot to disgrace me. It worked; the ninja grandmaster had me expelled, and, as Saki planned, he himself became the new head of the academy. He must have begun training his Foot Clan ninja soon after that—an army of evil warriors who live to obey his every command."

Leonardo nodded. "Fortunately we know that the Foot ninja are in Dimension X at the moment, and it doesn't look like Krang, the Dimension X warlord, is in any hurry to beam them back to Earth."

"Maybe that's because he doesn't want the Shredder to have a private army," suggested Donatello.

"Or perhaps he's just waiting for the right moment," said Splinter. "I have a suspicion that we may soon find out. Now, strap yourselves in; the instruments show that we're over Florida."

As the Turtles buckled their seat belts, Splinter pushed the joystick gently forward. It felt like being in an elevator going down very fast as the airship began its descent. Streamers of cloud scudded past the portholes, and the streetlights loomed up out of the darkness toward them.

"Do we have to go down so fast?" complained Raphael, who was not fond of flying.

"In order to avoid the Space Center radar, yes," said Splinter curtly. "We need to get very low very quickly. Now, please be silent, all of you." He stared out into the darkness. "I must estimate where the ground is."

"Urk," whispered Michaelangelo, clutching his midriff as the airship accelerated downward. "I think my last meal's doing backflips in my belly, guys."

"Here, Mike," said Leonardo, handing him a sickbag. "Take this."

Michaelangelo took it enthusiastically and peered inside. "What's this? Hey, it's empty!" he said, disappointed. "I thought you were giving me the last slice of a pizza, Leo."

"You didn't stay airsick for long!" said

Leonardo, chuckling. He peered out the window. "Hey, guys, check this out."

Outside in the moonlight they could see the outer fence of the Space Center. Armed soldiers trudged up and down, scanning the horizon for signs of any intruders. Inside, beyond a cluster of buildings, a rocket jutted up imposingly from the launchpad. It was illuminated by dozens of searchlights, so that its silver surface glittered almost as brightly as in the daylight. Technicians were swarming over the gantry around it, making checks and double checks, oblivious of the time of night.

Splinter was maneuvering the airship into the lee of a ridge, which concealed it from prying eyes. Having fallen like a rock, he slowed its descent drastically in the last hundred yards and touched down with just a gentle bump.

"Dream landing, master," Leonardo complimented him. He opened the hatch and beckoned the others to follow him out.

After locking the controls, Splinter also disembarked. "I will be coming with you," he said. "The Shredder is too dangerous to trifle with."

Raphael had scrambled up to the top of the ridge. "The base looks very well guarded," he said. "How are we going to get in?"

"First things first," admonished Splinter as he broke a few branches off a nearby tree and carried them over to the airship. "First we must camouflage our vessel in case anybody wanders this way."

A few minutes later, with the airship properly hidden under a covering of leafy branches, the Turtles began to creep toward the base. Suddenly they realized that Splinter was not with them and, looking around, they saw him heading in the opposite direction.

"Uh, master," said Donatello. "The base is this way."

Splinter barely glanced back as he beckoned them to follow him. "Remember your ninja training," he said as they caught him up. "The indirect approach is very often the best. As in this case. . ."

They reached the shoreline and made their way along it until they came across an outlet pipe. "It must connect to the Space Center's drains!" said Donatello.

Raphael pinched his nose and leaned forward into the darkness inside the pipe. "Phew, I'll say it does."

"Looks like there's room to go along it," said Leonardo, "though it'll be a tight squeeze."

"As a sewer rat I'm used to such environments," said Splinter. "I'll go first." He ducked into the pipe and was swallowed up by the blackness.

"Hey, slow down, master; wait for us," called Michaelangelo as he followed. His voice howled eerily along the metal pipe.

"Go on, Mike," said Raphael, giving him a shove. "Haven't you ever heard an echo before?" A moment later, as he, too, entered the pipe, he changed his tune. "Hmm, it is pretty creepy in here, isn't it?" he breathed.

Donatello drew out a pencil-thin flashlight from his belt. It cast a beam only about a yard ahead of them, but that was better than nothing. With Leonardo bringing up the rear, they began to advance.

"Will you quit shoving!"

"Get your elbow out of my face."

"Ouch, that was my toe!"

"Quiet!" hissed Leonardo. "Our voices carry a long way down this pipe—maybe as far as the base itself. A fine bunch of ninja you guys are!"

"Yeah," sniggered Raphael. "Imagine what that'd sound like. Some poor guy probably just jumped off the toilet because he thought it was talking to him!"

"This way," Splinter's voice echoed back to them from a point where the pipe forked. They followed in relative silence now, knowing that they must be directly underneath the base. Donatello was scanning the top of the pipe for a grille or inlet. As a result his flashlight beam was not directed ahead of them.

Michaelangelo walked straight into Splinter's back, and amid grunts and whispered swear words the others collided with him. "What is it, master?" he whispered. "Why have you stopped?"

"Stay very still, all of you," warned Splinter through gritted teeth. "Donatello, would you point that beam just ahead of me, please?"

Donatello complied, and there was a sharp intake of breath from all of them as the flashlight picked out a hulking figure in the darkness. Standing facing Splinter, he was jammed into the pipe with barely room to move. His skin was gray-green, thick and gnarled, and his long crocodile jaws were filled with sharp, curved fangs.

"Leatherhead!" gasped Michaelangelo.

Splinter pressed back as Leatherhead's massive jaws gaped wide. It wasn't that he was afraid, but Leatherhead had appalling bad breath. "Who?" he asked.

"I am Leatherhead!" announced the crocodile-man in a guttural voice.

"We fought him once before, master," explained Raphael. "He used to be a human, but he was changed into this form by a transmo . . . by a transmat . . . oh, by some weird gadget."

Leatherhead gave a great roar that rattled the wall of the pipe. "Turtles," he said. "I remember you. You are enemies of the Shredder."

"Yeah, that's right, buster," said Michaelangelo, leaning past Splinter, "and you don't much like the Shredder after he tried to trick you, as I recall. Well, he's right here and—"

"I know that!" growled Leatherhead. "He brought me along to help him, but he told me to hide down here in the sewer when I'm not needed. Now it looks like that was a lucky choice of hiding place, because it's brought you five straight into my jaws."

Splinter barely flinched as Leatherhead's grinning snout pressed forward. "Your attitude hardly seems rational," he said calmly. "Why work for the Shredder if he tricked you before?"

"He's promised to turn me back into a human being," snapped Leatherhead.

"And you believed him?" said Raphael. "Boy, Leatherhead is hardly the word: you should be called *Cloth*head. You've got less brains in you than an alligator-skin handbag!"

"Yeah, you make Bebop and Rocksteady look like the winners of *Jeopardy*," put in Donatello.

"I know what you're trying to do," said Leatherhead with a huge, cold grin. "You're trying to make me lose my temper so I do something dumb; but it won't work. . . . Hmm, now, I must say that I'd rather have turtle for starters and then rat to finish, but I guess I'll just have to take you as I find you."

"Let me past, master," pleaded Michaelangelo, anxious for his teacher's safety.

"I am in no danger, thank you, Michaelangelo," replied Splinter evenly, drawing a kusari-gama from his robe. This was no practice weapon, but the real thing. He brandished the shaft, which ended in a scythe blade, and allowed the iron ball to swing freely on its chain.

"Huh!" snorted Leatherhead. "What're you going to do with that, tunnel rat? It won't even pierce my hide."

Splinter just smiled. "Nor do I want it to. I get no pleasure from inflicting injury on dumb animals."

At this, Leatherhead gave a roar of rage. Suddenly Splinter jerked back his hand and the kusari-gama ball swung around to strike Leatherhead right on the snout. It did not seriously hurt him, but it caused his eyes to water with pain.

"Crocodile tears?" said Splinter. "Maybe you're upset at the thought of what an ugly thing you are."

This taunt was the last straw for Leatherhead. Bellowing ferociously, he opened his jaws and lunged forward, intending to bite Splinter in half. But the ninja master was as agile as he was wise, and he effortlessly dodged the clumsy attack of his tear-blinded opponent. Leatherhead's teeth snapped shut on thin air, and the next instant Splinter had wound the kusari-gama chain securely around his snout.

"That will hold him," Splinter told his pupils. "Crocodiles have great strength when it comes to biting, but the muscles for opening the jaw are much weaker."

"Wow, master," said Michaelangelo, peering past him at the struggling saurian, "where'd you learn that? Is it part of your advanced ninja education?"

"No, Michaelangelo, I actually saw it in an old *Tarzan* film that was on TV last week."

Leatherhead was wrenching his bulk around desperately in an attempt to get his hands on Splinter, but the pipe was too narrow for him to maneuver easily. Before he could back away, Splinter had blown a cloud of ninja sleeping-dust in his face, and in moments he was snoring soundly.

"That will keep him quiet while we clamber past," said Splinter, squeezing over the back of the sleeping reptile.

"Gee, master," said Donatello as the Turtles followed. "Should we just leave him here?"

"He is but a poor, misguided beast," was Splinter's reply. "It is the Shredder's lies that made him fight us, and the Shredder who is our true enemy. Therefore let us find him—and quickly, before his wicked plans come to fruition."

"What'd the master say?" whispered Leonardo, who, being at the back, was finding it hard to follow everything.

"He said we're off to clobber the Shredder," replied Donatello. "Hey, look!"

The flashlight beam had located a grating set into the pipe above their heads. It was the work of only a few seconds to wrench it free and climb through.

"I'm gonna need to bathe in deodorant for a week after this," said Michaelangelo with a groan as he emerged into the clean air.

"The express drain, I call it," said Raphael. "It's really the only way to travel."

They had emerged in an area at the

back of the Space Center kitchens, obviously adjoining the sentry barracks. Presumably the slops were thrown down into the sewers from here after mealtimes.

"I'm glad we didn't take the other fork, back there," muttered Donatello. "I dread to think where that would have brought us out."

The room was deserted and only dimly lit by a glimmer of light through a glass panel set over the door. Splinter was already at the door, listening intently. After a pause he signaled that the coast was clear, and they filed silently out into the corridor beyond.

"What now?" asked Leonardo.

Splinter motioned for him to keep his voice down. "We must find the buildings adjoining the launchpad," he said. "The astronauts will be billeted there. Hopefully we may even take Saki—I mean, the Shredder—unawares."

"Great!" said Michaelangelo. "I like that. We'll nab the twerp while he's napping."

"I doubt it'll be that easy, Mike," said Donatello. "It said in the paper that the rocket was due to lift off just after dawn. That's barely two hours away now, so the astronauts are bound to be in their space suits and ready to go."

"I agree," said Splinter, cautiously advancing along the passage to another door. "But we must try to confront the Shredder when he is on his own if possible. Otherwise there is a danger that innocent people could get hurt in the fighting."

Hearing nothing on the other side of the door, they edged it open and looked out across the Space Center. Searchlights set on the top of high guard towers swept routinely back and forth. A couple of sentries were visible about a hundred yards away, strolling along the well-lit perimeter wire. The rocket and its launch tower were some three hundred yards away, the soot of previous lift-offs stretching out in streaks from its base like the lines of a giant inkblot. Another cluster of buildings—all like the mess hall they were in, heavily shielded bunkers built to withstand the explosive energy of a rocket's blast—stood some way beyond the rocket.

"Those must be the astronauts' quarters," said Splinter. "That is where the other fork in the pipe might have taken us."

"I don't feel like going back down," said Raphael with a glance over his shoulder. "Leather-chops might have woken up and gotten himself free by now."

"Getting past the perimeter wire was the major problem," said Splinter, nodding. "We can easily cross the base from here without being spotted." He gestured at various jeeps and packing crates scattered around the launchpad. "We'll have ample cover."

They started out across the base toward the astronauts' quarters, carefully skirting the searchlight beams playing across the launchpad, darting into cover behind a jeep or packing case whenever one came too close. It took them almost half an hour to cross the three hundred yards to the rocket, but they made it without being spotted. Then their luck ran out.

A soldier emerged from behind a support strut of the launch tower. He had an automatic rifle slung casually across his shoulder. Seeing the Turtles and their master, he gaped in astonishment, bringing his rifle up by reflex.

Michaelangelo acted first. Rolling forward, he pulled three shuriken spikes from his belt and flung them at the sentry. The man put up one arm to shield his face, making his gun swing wildly. Bullets peppered the ground only inches from where the Turtles were standing.

"Stand back," Splinter ordered his pupils. Leveling a pipe, he spat a dart, which pierced the soldier's neck. He slapped at it as though it were a wasp sting, then seconds later crumpled to the ground.

The gunfire had already alerted other soldiers. Sirens began to blare all across the base. "Quickly," said Splinter. "We cannot reach the astronauts' quarters now. Follow me." He headed for the launch tower.

Leonardo paused beside the fallen guard. "Master—?" he said, hardly daring to inspect the motionless form.

"It was just a mild anesthetic, Leonardo," Splinter called back. "You know that I would never harm an innocent man. He'll come around within a minute—but he won't remember anything that happened in the last half hour. Including seeing us."

Leonardo joined the others, and they began to scramble up the scaffolding of the launch tower. The elevator would have been quicker, but they did not want to attract the attention of the other soldiers who were rushing to the scene. A jeep pulled up with screeching brakes, and they looked down to see a group of paratroopers jump out. They checked the

soldier whom Splinter's dart had stunned, then shone flashlights around them. They did not think to look up.

"Oh, this is just great," said Raphael with a groan. "We're left clinging to the launch tower like a bunch of underripe tomatoes. What do we do now?"

"Yes, master," said Donatello. "We'll never reach the Shredder now without being spotted; there are soldiers swarming all over the place."

"One thing's for sure," said Leonardo. "We can't stay where we are till it's light, or we'll certainly get caught."

Splinter ruminated for a moment, then nodded decisively and continued climbing.

"Wait, master," called Michaelangelo as quietly as he could. "Where are you going?"

"There is only one course of action left to us," Splinter replied. "We must go up into space with the Shredder and foil his plans there."

"You mean—?" gasped Michaelangelo.

Splinter nodded. "Precisely. We have to stow away aboard the shuttle."

Huddled in a storage locker on board the shuttle *Galileo,* the five of them watched dawn break through the cabin window. At the moment, the craft was pointing directly upward—not the direction for normal flight—but in the locker it hardly made any difference. The cramped space was not designed for comfort, in any case.

"We must've been here two hours already," said Raphael. "Aww, Mike, will you get your elbow out of my right ear, for crying out loud?"

"Sorry, Raph, but I can't reach your left ear from here."

A clang of footsteps sounded from the gantry outside, followed a few moments later by voices. Three men were coming aboard. But were they the astronauts— or soldiers looking for the Turtles? The five held their breath.

"Major Nelson, Major West, will you start the prelaunch check, please?" said one of the three. Even without the tinny distortion that usually accompanied his words, the Turtles recognized that voice. It belonged to their sworn enemy, the Shredder.

They heard various switches being tested as the two other astronauts reported the results of their check. Peering out through a crack in the locker door, Donatello could just make out the Shredder's broad back as he ticked off points on a clipboard. He told the others what he could see. Finally the check finished, and Major Nelson radioed the all-clear to Mission Control.

"This is bad," whispered Splinter. "I was hoping the Shredder would come aboard before the other two. We might have had the chance to overpower him and wring a confession out of him before the others arrived."

"It is a problem," agreed Leonardo. "How can we be sure of taking out the Shredder without the other two guys getting hurt in the process?"

"I think I might have a plan," piped up Michaelangelo.

"You?" the others chorused in disbelief. Usually Michaelangelo's mind was more on his next meal than on tactical planning.

The astronauts were buckling in for lift-off. "I think I'll have to wait to tell you till we're in orbit," whispered Michaelangelo. "Hang on to your hats, dudes, 'cause I think she's going up!"

An echo rang softly through the hull as explosive bolts jettisoned the cables linking the rocket to the launch tower. The noise of muffled sirens could be heard from all across the base warning stragglers to get to cover before the ignition sequence started. Over the cabin radio they heard the last part of the countdown: ". . . 10-9-8-7-6-5-ignition-3-2-1-0; lift-off, we have lift-off at seventeen minutes past the hour. You're looking good, boys, like a second sunrise."

"We read you, Control. Hope you brought your tanning oil, in that case," replied Major West. He was speaking through gritted teeth as the enormous force of the acceleration pressed all of them down hard. It was as if everyone weighed eight times more than normal. Without harnesses or padded seats, it was doubly uncomfortable for the hidden ninja in their tiny locker. Fortunately the worst of the G-force lasted only a half minute or so.

As the pressure eased, Nelson leaned over the mike. "We confirm first stage to detach in T minus ninety-seven seconds," he said after glancing over the instruments.

"Control, this is Munro," broke in the Shredder's voice. "I'll be feeding in the course corrections to shipboard computers just as soon as the burn's over. Will you double-check that we're still due to rendezvous with Orbital Platform II in an hour and a half?"

"Roger, *Galileo*," came the voice over the radio. "We can get it more accurate than that. The guys aboard Orbital tell me your coffee will be waiting at 3:43 precisely. Oh . . . and they say, one lump or two?"

West and Nelson laughed, joined after a calculating half-second by the Shredder's own feigned laughter. Like most villains, he had no sense of fun.

Inside the locker Splinter and the Turtles were just managing to disentangle themselves. "I feel like a beanbag," said Michaelangelo with a groan.

"That's a change—usually you feel like a pizza," said Leonardo. "Now, what's this plan you were talking about?"

"Well, you see . . ." whispered Michaelangelo; everybody huddled closer to hear him. ". . . You see, I thought we could call out for a delivery and jump the Shredder when he goes to the hatch to get it. . . . No, no, just kidding, guys!" he cried, grinning weakly as they glared at him. "This is the real plan . . ."

After Michaelangelo explained his idea, Donatello took another peek out into the cabin. Above them now, instead of the orange dawn of a Florida sky, only the deep blue of the upper atmosphere was visible outside the window. As he watched, stars began to appear with crystal clarity as the sky darkened into blackness. They were above the Earth's atmosphere, in outer space. The spacecraft juddered as the last stage of the rocket fell away and, as it did so, the acceleration stopped altogether. All weight left them, and they bobbed, lighter than feathers, inside the shuttle.

"How's that for a crash diet?" said Raphael. "I must've lost about a hundred and twenty pounds in sixty seconds."

"Raph," said Leonardo, wincing, "I wish you wouldn't use the word *crash*— at least not till we're back on firm ground!"

Donatello allowed a few seconds to get used to the weightless condition, then cautiously swung the locker door open. The three astronauts—or rather the two astronauts and the imposter—were all intent on their instrument readings. They failed to notice the four Turtles and their master slip quietly out of hiding and drift, swimmerlike, along the companionway to the aft cabin.

"Right, let's get to work," said Splinter when he was sure they were out of earshot of the three men up front. Obediently Donatello clawed his way over to a service panel and, removing it, got to work with a screwdriver. Donatello was the group's electronics wizard; he could do more with one screwdriver than most people could with an entire toolbox.

"I'm still not sure about this," said Leonardo, keeping a weather eye trained on the companionway.

"Yeah," agreed Raphael, looking at Michaelangelo. "Even if Don can get the wiring to go on the fritz, how do we know that it's the Shredder who'll come back here to take a look? He might send one of the others."

"Bah," said Michaelangelo, returning Raphael's dubious expression with his own black look. "You guys are just sore because you didn't think of a plan and I did."

"It *is* pretty unusual, Mike, you've got to admit," said Donatello from where he drifted, hunched up, over the access panel. He had his tongue pressed between his teeth as he concentrated on his work.

"It will work," said Splinter with his customary tone of absolute certainty. "The Shredder needs those other two to pilot the shuttle. He may have disguised himself to look like the real Colonel

Munro, but even he couldn't simulate an astronaut's rigorous training in just a few weeks."

Even as he spoke, there was a crackle of sparks and Donatello jumped back from the panel. He spun twice in midair before steadying himself by catching hold of a bulkhead rung. "Bingo," he said.

They heard a curse from the forward cabin. 'We've lost the radio,' said a voice; it sounded like Major West. There was a pause as he scanned the instrument panel. "The system's shorted out in aft bay, panel seven."

"I'll go back to check it out," said the Shredder. After a moment the Turtles heard him making his way hand-over-hand along the rungs lining the companionway.

Splinter gestured for them to remain silent and get into position. Leonardo stepped to one side of the hatch and, steadying himself with one hand against the bulkhead, began to swing the other, ready for a crashing bolo punch.

The hatch began to swing open.

Leonardo grinned widely. *Man, this is just so easy,* he thought. *I've always wanted to plant one right on the Shredder's nose. He won't even know what hit him.* . . .

5

The hatch had opened just a crack, then there was a long pause. Rigid with anticipation, they waited for the Shredder to enter. Finally they heard him call back to the flight deck: "There's nothing I can do to fix it right now. It'll have to wait until we've rendezvoused with the Orbital Platform." He allowed the hatch to close and moved off down the companionway.

"Unfortunately," Splinter whispered to his pupils, "it seems as though the Shredder doesn't particularly mind the radio being out of action."

"Figures," said Donatello, glaring at the charred tangle of wires protruding from the access panel. "Maybe I can short out something that he *will* care about."

Leonardo shook his head. "No. There's no telling what might happen if we keep on meddling with the shuttle's equipment."

"Hey," protested Donatello. "You call it meddling; *I* call it careful adjustment."

"Shush!" warned Raphael, who was listening at the hatch leading to the companionway. "The Shredder hasn't gone all the way up front yet."

He inched the hatch open and took a wary peek. The Shredder was floating in the companionway, at the midpoint between the flight deck and the aft cabin. As Raphael watched, he drew a strange gadget out of his overalls. It consisted of a handle beneath what looked like a miniature television, about the size of a walkie-talkie. The Shredder twisted a dial and the screen fizzed into life, swirling with colors for an instant before a gruesomely inhuman face became visible. Raphael strained his ears to catch what was said.

"Krang," said the Shredder. "There is some interference. Are you receiving me?"

The picture juddered with static, and a ghastly bubbling voice crackled out: "Who are you?"

The Shredder looked exasperated, but managed to force a grin. "It's me, Krang—Saki; you know, the Shredder."

"Saki! I didn't recognize you without your mask on." Krang's hideous face split in a toothy grin, and greenish spittle drooled down the corner of his mouth. "Have you anything to report on the progress of our plan?"

"It's all going fine," confirmed the Shredder in a hushed voice, turning down the volume on his communicator so that Majors Nelson and West would not overhear Krang's high-pitched rantings. Raphael risked creeping out into the companionway. He was counting on the Shredder not turning around—which was a gamble, but was the only way he could get to learn the plan.

"Don't worry about the interference, Saki," rasped Krang. "That will just be radiation from the Van Allen belts. It may also affect the shuttle's radio for a time."

"A wrench couldn't affect the shuttle's radio," chuckled the Shredder sinisterly. "It shorted out a few minutes ago."

"Perfect! Even if those fools on board with you realized that anything was afoot, they can't warn anyone."

The Shredder nodded. "A lucky stroke certainly. Speaking of things being afoot, are my Foot Clan ninja ready for action?"

"Indeed they are." Krang gestured with a vestigial tentacle, and the view displayed on the communicator changed temporarily. It now showed ranks of black-clad ninja standing at attention. Then the picture changed back to show Krang's alien face. "They are waiting in the transporter bay. You have only to get aboard the Orbital Platform with the teleport device I gave you, and I can beam your Foot soldiers directly there from Dimension X!"

The Shredder fairly rubbed his hands in glee. "Excellent. We'll have taken over the place before the fools even realize we've arrived."

"Hey, Colonel Munro?" Major Nelson called back from the flight deck. "Do I hear voices back there? Don't tell me we have a stowaway."

There was a glare of anger in the Shredder's eyes as he snapped off the communicator—like the expression of a cat who is disturbed while playing with a mouse. Then he forced a jovial laugh. "No, Major; I'm just talking to myself. I must be getting stir-crazy already."

Raphael watched the Shredder drift

forward to the flight deck, then silently backed up to join the others. He quickly told them what he had overheard.

"This is terrible," said Splinter. "I dread to think what would happen if the Shredder got control of that Orbital Platform. He could hold it and the crew aboard it for a ransom of millions of dollars."

"Imagine if he mounted laser weapons on it," said Donatello with a shudder. "That'd be a real Star Wars scenario."

Leonardo was all for jumping the Shredder right there and then. "Maybe you could get him with one of those knockout darts, master," he suggested to Splinter.

Splinter shook his head. "He is certain to be familiar with the drug used. Like any good ninja, he will have developed his resistance to it over the years."

"And the ballistics of blowguns or anything like that get pretty complicated in weightless conditions," added Donatello. "The only way we could be sure of getting him would be in hand-to-hand combat."

"So?" said Raphael. "Let's go!"

Splinter caught his arm as he drifted toward the hatch. "Do not be so impetuous, Raphael," he said. "A scuffle on the flight deck might easily damage the shuttle's control systems. We could end up flying off helplessly into space or crashing back to Earth."

"I don't want to end up as pavement pizza!" said Michaelangelo. "There must be something we can do."

"We'll have to wait until the shuttle makes its rendezvous with the Orbital Platform," said Splinter. "Without radio contact they won't attempt to dock. We can grab the Shredder when he space-walks over."

Suddenly they noticed that there was no sound of voices from the flight deck. Raphael gingerly eased open the companionway hatch. A soft hissing sound could be heard, eerily breaking the silence.

It was Donatello, of course, who first realized what it was. "The airlock!" he shouted. "The Shredder's already gone outside!"

Pushing themselves forward in the zero gravity, they swam up to the forward cabin. Nelson and West, the two real astronauts, were drifting limply above their seats, limbs swaying like seaweed.

"Are they . . . ?" asked Leonardo, taking a deep breath, as Splinter searched for a pulse.

"They're all right," said the rat master of ninjutsu with a sigh of relief. "The Shredder must have drugged their coffee, that's all." He nodded toward two cartons floating around the cabin.

Beyond the cabin window the imposing sight of the Orbital Platform drew their eyes. It had been constructed in space over a period of years: a vast, slowly rotating wheel of gantrywork fitted with bristling arrays of aerials and telescopes. Scientists worked six-month tours of duty up here in the lonely stillness of space, observing distant stars with a clarity that Earth's turbulent atmosphere did not allow on the ground. Several laboratory pods were connected to the great wheel, giving a total crew of perhaps thirty men. Even at a distance of eight hundred yards some of them were visible through the brightly lit portholes of the platform.

The Shredder was also visible, slowly drifting across the gulf of nothingness using a compressed-air pack for propulsion. He had Krang's teleport device clipped to his belt. Lights winked on beside one of the platform's airlocks.

"They're going to let him go aboard!" said Donatello with a gasp. "Talk about inviting a viper into the nest . . ."

"Don't forget, they think that he is the real Colonel Munro," said Splinter. "Quickly—get into space suits. We must apprehend him before he reaches the platform."

There was a problem. The *Galileo*'s stores only contained two other space suits. Neither was a particularly good fit for a mutant turtle.

Knowing that Raphael and Michaelangelo were the most agile of his students, Splinter directed them to put on the two suits. By tying string around the trousers and sleeves, which were way too long, they managed to improvise a passable fit. All the same, they looked like Laurel wearing Hardy's hand-me-downs.

"Haw, haw," chortled Donatello.

"*Very* funny," said Raphael.

"Cowabunga, we're going into space, you guys!" said Michaelangelo delightedly. "What a radical experience."

"Just make sure your suits don't get torn," warned Donatello as he handed them compressed-air packs. He had set the nozzles for maximum thrust to give them a chance of overtaking the Shredder. "And aim the jets carefully. These packs only give a total of sixty seconds' thrust. If you overshoot the Shredder, you'll drift off into space forever."

Raphael and Michaelangelo got into

the airlock. "Wow, I feel like Luke Sky-walker off to tackle Darth Vader" was Mike's last remark as the door slid shut behind them.

A moment later they appeared out-side. Peering through the cabin window, hardly daring to breathe, the others watched them kick off and drift in pur-suit of the Shredder. He did not seem to have noticed them yet, at least, so he was not particularly hurrying to reach the platform.

"Don," said Leonardo, "what happens if their suits get ripped? Can't they just hold their breath till they get back in-side?"

"I'm afraid not," said Donatello sol-emnly. "The minute the suit gave way, they'd be exposed to the vacuum of space. The drop in pressure would kill them instantly!"

The two Turtles were gaining on their foe, but they had not reckoned on the platform's crew. A group of technicians standing at a porthole saw the man they assumed to be Colonel Munro heading toward the station with two rather outlandish figures in hot pursuit. When the figures drew a little closer and the technicians saw their green reptilian faces, it brought to mind images of Martians from old science fiction films. They immediately began waving furiously to attract "Munro's" attention.

The Shredder saw them waving, but at first he only curled his lip in contempt. "The fools," he muttered to himself. "What do they think they're doing—waving hello? I'll give them a greeting they'll never forget, once I teleport my Foot soldiers aboard!"

As he approached the airlock, it was obvious that the technicians were getting very excited about something. They pressed their faces close to the portholes and seemed to be trying to tell him something. Like all ninja, the Shredder excelled at lipreading. Watching one of the men, he spelled out what was being said: "Behind you!"

The Shredder twisted around. Raphael and Michaelangelo were only ten yards away, and closing in fast. "You Turtles!" he snarled. "Isn't there *anywhere* that I can away from you?"

Since the helmet radios were not

switched on, they could not hear him. Michaelangelo replied using ninja sign language, made clumsily slurred by the bulky gloves: "Give up, Shred; we're on to you."

The Shredder understood the message, but ignored it. Raising his hand, he buffeted Raphael on the side of the helmet as they closed in on him. Both he and Raphael recoiled, spinning apart from the collison, and Michaelangelo tackled him.

The others were watching from the shuttle. "Raphael's going off into deep space!" cried Donatello in alarm. "Raph, use your jet pack."

Raphael had no way of hearing this warning—unless long comradeship meant that the Turtles shared some kind of telepathy. Nonetheless he managed to turn his pack around and used a burst of air to brake his motion. Gradually he maneuvered back to where Michaelangelo and the Shredder were struggling.

If the Shredder had been wearing his

knife-gauntlets, the fight would have been over in seconds—he could have easily sliced open his enemy's space suit. As it was, the two of them were forced to rely on pure unarmed combat skills. The contest still favored the Shredder, who was individually more than a match for any of the Turtles, except that he had not fully recovered from the surprise of seeing his old foes up here in space. Also, Michaelangelo had some practice in fighting underwater. It was not exactly like the weightlessness of space, but it gave him a slight edge to compensate for the Shredder's superior strength and skill. He grabbed the Shredder's arm and tried to twist it in a lock behind his back. The Shredder responded with a round-house punch, which lost most of its impact because of the lack of gravity; the main effect was to set them both spinning like tops.

Moments later Raphael careened into the fray, and all three of them began to tumble out of control, away from the Orbital Platform.

"Oh no, they're falling toward the earth's atmosphere," realized Donatello. He knew that, without the protection of a spaceship's heat shield, they would burn up in seconds on reentry.

To make matters worse, the Shredder had managed to direct the nozzle of his propulsion pack at Michaelangelo. As they struggled, he released a blast of compressed air. The effect was to rocket him and Raphael toward the Orbital Platform, while Michaelangelo shot even faster away toward the looming Earth.

"Mike!" screamed Raphael. Panic and horror made him release his grip on the Shredder, who lost no time in heading back toward the platform. This time he made it without incident, and the airlock door slid open to admit him.

Michaelangelo was falling so fast that Raphael had no chance to reach him. Sick at heart, he used the last of his jet pack's charge to return to the *Galileo*. As he came aboard, he found Donatello already feverishly working the controls.

Leonardo and Splinter were trying to wake the drugged astronauts.

"Do you think you can fly this thing, Don?" asked Raphael as he discarded his space helmet.

Donatello answered distractedly. "I'm going to have to. We can't let Mike die, even though that means letting the Shredder carry out his evil scheme."

"It would help if we could bring the regular pilots around," said Leonardo. "How about it, master?"

Splinter shook his head. "No, they are sound asleep and may remain so for hours yet. It is all up to Donatello now."

"I was afraid you'd say that," muttered Donatello. "Well, nothing really compares with learning by doing. Here goes!" With that he depressed a lever, and the force of the thrusters throbbed through the *Galileo*'s hull. Taking the control column, he began to swing the shuttle around.

Raphael was peering forlornly out the porthole. "You've got to hurry!"

The shuttle took only half a minute to turn around, but it seemed like unbearable ages to them. Finally, his sights set on his brother's flailing figure dead ahead, Donatello kicked in the full thrust. Everyone was thrown back as the shuttle accelerated in pursuit, speeding toward the blue globe of the Earth like a silver javelin.

"Donatello, you will have to match Michaelangelo's velocity exactly," said Splinter. "Raphael, here is a rope. Get fully suited up again and get into the airlock; you must be ready to pull Mike aboard." Splinter sounded calm, but the others could tell that he must be very worried indeed; normally he would never use the shortened version of their names.

The planet came rushing up toward them like a whirlpool of blue in the midst of an infinite black sea. Michaelangelo had receded to a tiny cartwheeling speck, but now they could at least see that they were gaining on him. There was no time to lose: he was already enveloped in a halo of pale light as he began to skim the atmosphere.

Raphael had already taken up position in the open airlock. As the *Galileo* drew alongside his falling friend, he could feel the rise in temperature himself. At least Michaelangelo was still struggling, which was a good sign. *Probably yelling his lungs off like a fool as well, even though there's nobody up here who can hear him,* thought Raphael. He allowed himself a grim smile as he let out the rope. *Come on, Mike, grab it. Have you got your eyes closed, or what?*

In fact, it was getting very hot inside Michaelangelo's suit—worse than a steam bath. He was only half-conscious of what was happening. Dimly, as though a veil were being drawn back and forth across his eyes, he became aware of a trailing rope brushing his gloved hand. He tried to close his fingers around it, but the stifling heat made him pass out for a few seconds. When he came to, he tried weakly to remember where he was.

The idea that he might be drowning in the ocean came to him, but he was not worried. Turtles are at home underwater, after all. That was all right, then; he closed his eyes . . .

◆

"Glub." Michaelangelo came to as a cupful of cold water was flung into his face. No, it wasn't water. He licked his lips; it was Coke!

He opened his eyes to find the others peering down at him, smiles of relief on their faces. "Hey, what'd I tell you?" said Leonardo, who was holding a can of chilled cola from the shuttle's stores. "This Turtle is too cool to toast!"

Splinter laid a hand on Michaelangelo's arm. "Rest now, my son. We are all proud of you."

Michaelangelo's head was still swimming from the heat, but he managed to get shakily to his feet. "I'm fine, master, thanks," he said, "but I think you should have gone after the Shredder instead of saving me. Now that he's got aboard the Orbital Platform, it spells big trouble for everyone on Earth."

"I don't think so, dude," said Raphael. "You see, while we were struggling out there in space, I managed to filch these off his belt." Grinning in self-satisfaction, he held up the Shredder's communicator and teleport device.

"He won't be able to cause much trouble without his army of Foot soldiers," called back Donatello from the flight cabin. "And he won't even be able to get back to Earth until the next shuttle goes up."

"That will not be for several months," said Splinter. "However, in the meantime we have to return *this* shuttle safely back to its base. Donatello . . . ?"

"We're right on course, master. I'll take her in over the Bahamas, and then switch to automatic pilot. We can bail out just offshore, and the control tower will be able to fly her in to landing."

All went smoothly, and only a few hours later they were bobbing up and down in the sea watching the *Galileo* soar sleekly across the afternoon sky toward Cape Canaveral. Since Splinter was not as good a swimmer as the Turtles, he was perched on top of Leonardo's back, the Shredder's communicator tucked safely in his belt. The teleport device was still aboard the shuttle.

"I think the pilots were just waking up when we bailed out," said Donatello as they struck out toward the coast, "so they probably won't need to land under autopilot after all."

Michaelangelo chuckled; he was feeling much recovered from the refreshing dip. "I wonder what they'll make of it all, once everyone's told his story?"

"They have yet another surprise in store," said Splinter. He flicked on the communicator, but made sure it was set to transmit sound only. After a moment

Krang's bloated face appeared on the screen.

"What is it, Saki?" whined the alien warlord. "And why can't I see you?"

Splinter coughed and then spoke in a perfect imitation of the Shredder's imperious tones: "The radiation here in space must still be causing static. You told me that yourself."

"So I did," admitted Krang. "Well, how is the plan going?"

"Perfectly. I am aboard the Orbital Platform and I will set the teleporter in position in forty minutes' time. Be ready to beam my soldiers from Dimension X then."

"I will, I will," Krang cackled. "Excellent work, Saki. You have managed to do something right, for a change. Over and out."

"Now, that's what I call phoning ahead," said Raphael as Splinter switched off the communicator.

"Great plan, master," said Leonardo admiringly. "Those Foot ninja will be teleported slap-bang into the middle of the Cape Canaveral base!"

Splinter laughed. "Yes. The soldiers should arrest them on sight—so even when the Shredder gets back to terra firma, he won't have his private army anymore."

They were soon back aboard the Turtle airship and drifting lazily northward through the gathering night. Stars sparkled above them out of a clear sky. It seemed strange to think that they had been up in space themselves only hours ago.

"All in all, a pretty fair day's work, I'd say," announced Michaelangelo.

"And we should be getting home just around breakfast time," said Leonardo, glancing at the clock. "How about celebrating with a meal of fish and chips?"

Splinter groaned and handed him a five-dollar bill. "Here, Leonardo," he told him, "get pizzas instead. They cause much less trouble!"